# LITTLE CRITTER'S®
# THE
# FUSSY PRINCESS

### BY
### MERCER MAYER

A GOLDEN BOOK • NEW YORK
Western Publishing Company, Inc., Racine, Wisconsin 53404

One night Little Sister couldn't get to sleep. "I can't sleep without my fuzzy pink bear," Little Sister complained.

"You don't need your fuzzy pink bear to sleep!" Little Critter said sharply.

"I do, too," insisted Little Sister. "I need my bear or I can't sleep at all."

Little Critter sighed and went to get Little Sister's bear. He handed it to her and got back into bed.

"You are too fussy," Little Critter said.

"Did you say I was fuzzy?"
"No, fussy, fussy, fussy," said Little Critter.
"What does 'fussy' mean?" asked Little Sister.
"I'll tell you a story about a fussy princess, and then you'll know," answered Little Critter.
"Okay," said Little Sister.
Little Critter began to tell the story.

"Once upon a time, a long, long time ago, there was a fussy princess who couldn't sleep unless everything was just right. She had to have all her favorite dolls propped on the bed in just the right order. She had to have her favorite blanket, and the sheets had to be perfectly smooth."

Little Sister interrupted Little Critter. "You're telling a story about me. I don't like stories that are about me."

"Are you a princess who lived a long, long time ago?" asked Little Critter.

"Well, no," admitted Little Sister.

"Then this story is not about you," Little Critter explained. "So do you want to hear it or not?"

"All right, go on," said Little Sister.

"Here we go, then," said Little Critter. "This princess had to have everything just so at night. If the window was open too much, she had to have it shut. If the air was too still, someone had to fan her. And everyone in the castle had to be quiet and tippy-toe around after she went to bed, because the least little noise would disturb her.

"She was no picnic during the day, either. All of her dresses had to be perfectly pressed. If they had even the slightest wrinkle, she hollered and threw a fit. She had the royal maids ironing her clothes all day.

"Oh, and if she fell down, she screamed and screamed and screamed. There was nothing the royal baby-sitter, the royal clown, or the princess's very own parents could do to stop her from crying.

"One day a big dragon who lived in the mountains flew down to the castle. He had heard about the fussy princess and how the servants took care of her. It sounded like a good deal to him, and he liked the castle when he saw it. So he decided to move in.

"The first thing he did was throw out the king and his family. So the royal family had to spend the first night in a barn. The princess had to sleep with cows, donkeys, sheep, and chickens. Needless to say, she didn't sleep a wink, and in the morning she was in a very bad mood.

"When the farmer found them the next morning, he threw them out for trespassing. That night they had to sleep under a tree. Of course it rained, and the royal family got all wet. The princess didn't sleep well that night, either.

"By the third night the princess was a cranky mess. Her fur was matted with mud. Her new gown was wrinkled! This was just too much. Not only had her family been thrown out of the castle and forced to live under a tree, not only was her only dress ruined, but the dragon had her favorite blanket and all of her dolls. So she hollered and threw a fit. She yelled and screamed until her father promised to go and get her things from the dragon.

"Her father went back to the castle, pounded on the door, and told the dragon to open up. And that's just what the dragon did—he opened the door. Then he blew his fiery breath at the king and chased him away. The king went back to his family, under the tree, feeling defeated and slightly scorched.

"So the princess made up her mind to be brave. She decided to sneak into the castle that night when everyone was asleep and get her favorite dolls and blanket. It was very late when she reached the castle, so she sneaked upstairs to her room.

"The princess was very surprised to find the dragon asleep in her bed with her favorite blanket, and all her dolls propped around him. Boy, did she get mad. And even though there was a dragon in her bed, she was so angry, she wasn't even scared.

"The princess was so mad, she went to the laundry room and got a big bucket of soapy water. Then she went upstairs and threw it right in the sleeping dragon's face. The poor dragon woke up with a snort and a sputter.

"The dragon slowly got out of bed. He drew
himself up as tall as possible, glared at the princess
with his big yellow eyes, and showed her his fangs.
*Now* the princess was more scared than angry. She
started to back away toward the door. The dragon
puffed himself up and began to blow fire at her—
but all that came out were soapy bubbles.

"The dragon was shocked! The princess had put out his fire. No one had ever put out his fire before, and without his fire he couldn't be ferocious, let alone scary. So he sat down on the floor and cried and cried. Meanwhile the king and queen had discovered that the princess was missing. They thought she had gone back to the castle, so they ran there as fast as they could.

"Imagine how surprised the king and queen were to find their daughter comforting a crying dragon. Right then and there the princess decided not to be fussy anymore. After living under a tree, she realized it didn't matter if her favorite blanket wasn't in just the right spot, or if someone made a little noise when she was trying to sleep.

"The dragon was so moved by the princess's change of heart that he apologized for being so awful. And the king and queen were so happy, they invited the dragon to stay on as a house guest."

"Is that the story?" asked Little Sister.

"That's it," said Little Critter. "Now go to sleep."

"Well, now I *need* my fuzzy blanket, but your story has made me sleepy, so I think I'll go to sleep anyway." Little Sister yawned and snuggled under the covers.

"Good. And good night," said Little Critter, who also yawned and fell right asleep.